CARTER HIGH
SENIOR YEAR

SOMEONE TO
Count On

By Eleanor Robins

D1559953

SADDLEBACK
EDUCATIONAL PUBLISHING

CARTER HIGH
SENIOR YEAR

www.sdlback.com

ISBN-13: 978-1-61651-328-3
ISBN-10: 1-61651-328-4
eBook: 978-1-60291-976-1

Printed in Malaysia

20 19 18 17 16 4 5 6 7 8

Chapter 1

It was Wednesday. Cruz sat in the lunchroom. He ate lunch with Rey. Cruz was on the baseball team. Rey was on the team too.

Rey's real name was Reynardo. But his friends called him Rey.

Rey said, "The spring dance is next week."

"I know," Cruz said.

"Do you have a date for it?" Rey asked.

Cruz said, "Not yet. But I will as soon as I ask someone."

Cruz knew Rey didn't have a date to the dance. Rey and his girlfriend broke up. So Rey didn't have a girlfriend now.

"Who are you going to ask?" Rey asked.

"I don't know. I might ask Ana or Paz. Or I might ask someone else," Cruz said.

Then he laughed.

Rey said, "You better hurry and ask someone before it's too late. Then no one will go with you."

Cruz laughed.

Then he said, "I have a lot of time. Don't worry about me. I will have a date. But you might not have a date."

"You are right about that," Rey said.

"Who do you want to take?" Cruz asked.

Cruz didn't really care who Rey wanted to take to the dance. But he had to talk to Rey about something. And Cruz liked to talk about girls.

Rey said, "I want to take Nina."

Cruz knew Nina. She was in a class with him.

Cruz said, "You want to go with Nina. So you should ask her."

"I would ask her. But I don't see her much at school. And I don't have her phone number. So I can't call her," Rey said.

"Too bad. Maybe you will see her soon," Cruz said.

Rey said, "But a lot of boys like Nina. Someone might ask her before I see her. I need her phone number. But I don't know anyone who can get it for me."

"Nina is in a class with me. So I can get her number for you," Cruz said.

Rey seemed surprised.

He asked, "You would do that for me?"

"Sure. Why not? We are friends," Cruz said.

And Cruz didn't want to date Nina.

Rey said, "Thanks, Cruz. I am glad I have a friend I can count on. When do you have a class with her?"

"After lunch," Cruz said.

"I sure would like to have her phone number today. Then I could call her tonight. Can you get it for me today?" Rey asked.

"Sure I can," Cruz said.

"Will you bring it to baseball practice?" Rey asked.

"Sure," Cruz said.

It wasn't a big deal.

"Thanks, Cruz. But make sure Nina knows it is for me, not for you," Rey said.

"I will," Cruz said. Then he laughed.

Chapter 2

The school day was over. Cruz was on his way to baseball practice. But he wasn't in a hurry to get there. He didn't want to get there early. He might have to work harder.

Cruz stopped along the way to talk to some girls. Then he went on to practice. He made sure he got there on time.

He saw Rey and Al. They were throwing a ball to each other.

Al was Rey's best friend. His real name was Alberto. But his friends called him Al.

Al was OK. But Cruz didn't think Al liked him very much.

Rey stopped throwing the ball. He ran over to Cruz.

Rey said, "I thought you would never get here. Did you bring it?"

"What?" Cruz asked.

He brought himself. That was all he needed to bring.

Rey said, "Nina's phone number. You said you would get her phone number. You said you would bring it to me at practice."

"I did?" Cruz asked.

He had forgotten all about it. Cruz didn't want to date Nina. So it wasn't like he wanted her number for himself.

Rey looked upset. He said, "You said you would bring me Nina's number. And I thought I could count on you to bring it. You really didn't bring it?" Rey asked.

"No. I forgot to ask her," Cruz said.

Rey seemed mad.

"It isn't a big deal," Cruz said.

"It is to me. I wanted to call her tonight. And now I can't," Rey said.

"Nina is only one girl. So ask some other girl," Cruz said.

Cruz would if he were Rey.

"But I don't want to date some other girl. I want to date Nina," Rey said.

"So ask her tomorrow morning at school," Cruz said.

"I can't," Rey said.

Cruz laughed.

Then he asked, "Why? Are you afraid she will say no?"

Rey said, "No, Cruz. I told you. I don't see her much at school. So I might not see her tomorrow."

"Yeah. I forgot," Cruz said.

Rey didn't say any more. He ran back

over to Al. They started to throw a ball to each other again.

Rey was upset with Cruz. And Cruz didn't know what the big deal was. So he forgot to get Nina's phone number for Rey. She wasn't the only girl at Carter High. Rey could always ask someone else.

Chapter 3

It was the next day. Cruz was at school. He was on his way to class. He saw Paz. He had dated Paz a few times.

Paz smiled at him.

She said, "Hi, Cruz."

"Hi," Cruz said.

He stopped to talk to Paz. He was in no hurry to get to class.

Paz said, "I had fun on our last date, Cruz."

"So did I," Cruz said.

He knew Paz wanted him to say that.

He was ready to walk on down the hall. But maybe he should say something else to her.

"We will have to go out again, soon," Cruz said.

Paz said, "Yes. We will."

"I will call you. Maybe we can do something next week," Cruz said.

Paz said, "OK. The spring dance is next week. It should be very nice this year. I wanted to go to the spring dance with you last year, Cruz. But you asked me too late. And I already had a date."

Cruz said, "Yeah. Maybe we can go together this year. We need to talk about it. I will call you. But right now I have to get to class. So I need to hurry."

Cruz went on down the hall. But he didn't hurry.

Cruz got to his math class. Math was his best class. So he didn't have to work hard in the class. Most of the time he made an A or B.

But he was glad when class was over.

Cruz walked to his next class. He saw Ana in the hall. He dated Ana off and on for most of the year. But he dated other girls too. And she dated other boys.

"Cruz, I need to talk to you," Ana said.

Cruz stopped to talk to her.

"What about?" he asked.

"You said you would call last night. And you didn't call me. The spring dance is next Friday night. Are you taking me to the dance or not? I need to know, Cruz." Ana said.

Cruz didn't want to talk to Ana about the dance. He might ask her to the dance. He might ask Paz. Or he might ask someone else.

But he didn't have to be in a hurry to ask anyone. He knew Ana and Paz wanted to go with him. So they would wait for him to ask them.

"You know I always like to date you," Cruz said.

And he did like to date Ana. But he liked to date other girls too.

"I always like to date you too, Cruz. But what about the dance?" Ana asked.

"I will have to call you. Then we can talk about the dance. But I am in a hurry now. I have to get to class. So I don't have time to talk," Cruz said.

"OK, Cruz. But make sure you call me tonight," Ana said.

"I will," Cruz said.

Ana said, "I need to get to class too. Be sure to call me tonight, Cruz."

"I will," Cruz said.

Cruz went on down the hall. But he didn't hurry.

Cruz wasn't sure he wanted to take Ana to the dance. But now he might have to ask her. He liked her more than Paz. But he thought he might ask someone else.

That was OK. It was only a dance.

And he could always date someone else next week.

Chapter 4

The morning went by quickly for Cruz. He was on his way to lunch. He saw Rey. Rey was talking to a girl. Her name was Tia.

Tia was very pretty. And Cruz wanted to date her. But she had dated the same boy all year.

Tia was talking to Rey. Did Tia and her boyfriend break up? Was Rey trying to ask her out?

Tia stopped talking to Rey. She went in a classroom. Rey went on down the hall.

Cruz said, "Wait, Rey. I will walk to lunch with you."

Rey didn't stop walking.

Cruz thought Rey didn't hear him. So he hurried after Rey. Cruz caught up with him.

Rey didn't look glad to see Cruz.

The boys walked on down the hall to the lunchroom.

"What do you want, Cruz?" Rey asked.

Cruz said, "I saw you talking to Tia. Did Tia and her boyfriend break up?"

"Maybe they did. And maybe they didn't. But I am not going to tell you," Rey said.

That surprised Cruz very much.

"Why? Do you want to date her?" Cruz asked.

"No. I told you who I want to date. I want to date Nina," Rey said.

The boys got to the lunchroom. Then they went in.

"So tell me, Rey. Did Tia and her

boyfriend break up?" Cruz asked.

"I need to get my lunch," Rey said.

Rey got his tray. He walked away from Cruz. Then he went to a table and sat down.

Cruz got his tray. He went over the table. Then he sat down with Rey.

Rey didn't look glad that he did.

Cruz said, "So tell me, Rey. Did Tia and her boyfriend break up or not?"

Rey didn't answer him.

"You said you didn't want to date her. So why won't you tell me?" Cruz asked.

"I just don't want to tell you," Rey said.

"Why? I am not just anyone. I am your friend," Cruz said.

"Not anymore. I thought you were my friend, Cruz. I counted on you. But you let me down. I don't need a friend like you," Rey said.

That surprised Cruz.

Cruz asked, "Why? What did I do?"

"It's not what you did, Cruz. It's what you didn't do," Rey said.

"What are you talking about? What didn't I do?" Cruz asked.

Rey hadn't asked him to do anything.

"You said you would get Nina's phone number for me. But you didn't," Rey said.

"Are you still mad about that?" Cruz asked.

"No. But I don't want you as my friend anymore. I need to count on my friends," Rey said.

"You can count on me. I will get her phone number today. And I will bring it to you at practice. You can count on that," Cruz said.

And Cruz meant it. He would ask Nina for her phone number as soon as he saw her.

Rey said, "I don't need her phone

number now, Cruz. I saw Nina in the hall this morning. It was after my first class. I asked her to the dance. She already has a date."

"That is too bad," Cruz said.

Rey seemed mad.

Rey said, "Yes. It is too bad. Someone asked Nina before school this morning. So she didn't have a date last night. She might have said she would go with me then. But you didn't bring me her phone number. So I couldn't call her last night."

"Why are you so upset, Rey? Nina isn't the only girl at Carter High. You should ask someone else," Cruz said.

"Yes. I know. You told me that before," Rey said.

Then Rey got up. He picked up his tray. And he went to sit with someone else.

Cruz couldn't believe it. Rey was still mad about a girl's phone number.

Rey acted like Nina was the only girl in the school.

Cruz would ask someone else if he were Rey. Besides, he didn't want to date just one girl.

The afternoon went by quickly for Cruz. He was on his way to baseball practice. But he was in no hurry to get there.

Cruz saw Tia. He was sure she and her boyfriend had broken up. If they hadn't, Rey would have told him.

Cruz didn't think Tia would have a date to the dance yet. So he would ask her.

Cruz went over to Tia. She seemed surprised. She was glad to see him.

"Hi, Tia," he said.

"Hi," Tia said.

"Did you and your boyfriend break up?" Cruz asked.

"Yes," Tia said.

"Do you have a date for the spring dance?" Cruz asked.

Tia said, "Not yet. But I am not sure I will be here that night."

"Why?" Cruz asked.

"I might go out of town," Tia said.

"Do you have to go?" Cruz asked.

"No," Tia said.

"Then don't go. Stay in town. Go to the dance with me," Cruz said.

All of the other boys would want Tia to go with them. So Cruz wanted her to go with him too.

Tia said, "I want to go to the dance. But I don't know. I have already made plans to go out of town."

"So change them," Cruz said.

"I don't know. I will have to think about that," Tia said.

"OK. Think about it," Cruz said.

"But I still might go out of town. Is

it OK to let you know on Monday?" Tia asked.

"Sure," Cruz said.

Cruz wanted to know right then. But it was OK for him to find out next week. He wasn't worried. Tia wouldn't go out of town. Not when she could go to the dance with him.

Chapter 5

Cruz got to baseball practice. He was almost late.

Cruz looked over at Coach Karr. Coach Karr looked over at him. The coach didn't look pleased.

Was Coach Karr upset with him? Cruz didn't think the coach should be mad. He had just gotten to practice. He wasn't late. And he hadn't done anything to upset the coach.

Al ran over to him.

Al said, "You were almost late, Cruz."

"But I got here on time," Cruz said.

Al said, "Yes. But you need to come

early. You shouldn't wait until the last minute."

"You come when you want to come. And I will come when I want to come," Cruz said.

"We have a chance to be number one this year. And we all need to work hard," Al said.

Cruz never worked hard. He wanted to be on the team. But he didn't like to practice. He was only on the back-up team. But that was fine with him.

Al was on Team 1. So Al worked hard. But Cruz didn't want to be on Team 1. So he didn't need to come early. And he didn't need to work hard.

Coach Karr blew his whistle.

Then he said, "You won't have practice tomorrow. So work hard today. Play your best."

The boys practiced on their own for

a while.

Cruz did some exercises. Then he batted some balls.

Then Coach Karr said, "Get ready to play. Team 1 in the field first. Team 2 at bat first."

In the first inning, Cruz hit the ball. But he didn't run fast enough to beat out the throw to first base. So he made an out.

The first baseman said, "I am glad you didn't run fast, Cruz. Or you would have been safe."

Cruz laughed.

Then he said, "I know."

But he didn't need to run fast. It was not a real game.

In the third inning, Cruz hit a long ball. It could have been a triple. But Cruz didn't run very fast. So he got a double.

Cruz hit a home run later. But he

didn't hurry around the bases.

Cruz was glad when practice was over. He was ready to go home.

He walked off the field.

Coach Karr called to him.

Coach Karr said, "Cruz, come over here. We need to talk."

All of the boys looked at Cruz. Some of them started to laugh.

Were they laughing at him? Cruz didn't think they were. But he wasn't sure about that.

Cruz didn't know why Coach Karr needed to talk to him. He hadn't done anything wrong. His team didn't win the game. But they were only the back-up team.

And he was the only player to get a double. He also got a home run.

Cruz went over to Coach Karr. But he didn't hurry.

"What do we need to talk about, Coach?" Cruz asked.

"The team has a chance to do well this year. We might even be number one in the state," Coach Karr said.

Cruz already knew that. Was that all Coach Karr wanted to talk to him about?

Coach Karr said, "The team can do it. But all the players have to work hard. And that means you too, Cruz."

"I work hard," Cruz said.

But that wasn't true. And Cruz knew it.

Coach Karr said, "You never come early. So you can't do any extra work. Some days you are almost late. And you don't work hard when you get here."

"I work hard," Cruz said.

Then he laughed.

Coach Karr didn't look pleased at all.

Coach Karr said, "I need players I can count on. And I can't count on you, Cruz.

Don't come to practice again unless you plan to work hard."

That surprised Cruz very much. He couldn't believe Coach Karr said that to him.

Cruz laughed.

But Coach Karr didn't laugh.

Then Cruz asked, "Are you joking, Coach? You wouldn't really take me off the team? Would you?"

Coach Karr said, "Yes, Cruz. I would take you off the team. It is up to you. Plan to work hard or don't come to practice."

Cruz didn't want to work too hard. But he didn't want to be taken off the team either. He liked the girls to know he was on the baseball team.

"You can count on me, Coach. From now on I will work hard," Cruz said.

And maybe he would work hard. But Cruz wasn't so sure he would.

Chapter 6

Cruz didn't call Paz. And he didn't call Ana either. He didn't want to see them at school on Friday. So he hurried from class to class.

He didn't see Paz. But he did see Ana.

Ana waved at him. But she didn't ask him why he hadn't called her. And she didn't ask him about the dance. That surprised Cruz. But he was glad she didn't ask him.

Cruz was glad when Monday morning came. He was in front of the school. He looked for Tia. But he didn't see her.

He wanted to know about the dance.

Cruz was sure Tia would go with him.

He saw Rey and Al. Cruz walked over to them. Then the three boys walked toward the school.

Al said, "You need to work hard at practice, Cruz. Is that why Coach Karr wanted to talk to you?"

Cruz laughed.

Then Cruz asked, "Why would you think that? I work hard."

"No. You don't work hard. And Coach Karr should take you off the team. I would if I were him," Al said.

"So would I," Rey said.

Then Rey laughed.

Cruz didn't like it when the other boys laughed at him.

Cruz didn't think Coach Karr would take him off the team. But the coach might. He didn't want the other boys to laugh at him. So Cruz would work hard at practice. Cruz hoped Coach Karr wouldn't take him off the team.

Rey and Al talked about the spring dance. Rey had a date. But it wasn't with Nina.

"Who are you taking to the dance, Cruz?" Rey asked.

Cruz laughed.

Then he said, "I don't know yet. But I will have a date."

He knew that for sure.

Rey said, "It is a little late, Cruz. Are you sure you can get a date now?"

"Don't worry about me. I will have a date. You can count on that," Cruz said.

Then he laughed again.

He saw Tia. She was on her way in the school. And she was walking by herself.

Cruz said, "See you later. I have to go talk to my date."

Cruz called to Tia.

He said, "Wait, Tia."

She stopped and waited for him.

Cruz walked over to Tia. But he didn't hurry.

"How about it, Tia? Are you going to the dance with me?" Cruz asked.

But he already knew what she would say. She would say yes. He would have a date.

"Sorry, Cruz. But I can't go with you," Tia said.

Cruz couldn't believe she said that.

"What do you mean? Why can't you go with me?" Cruz asked.

"I told you I had plans to go out of town," Tia said.

"But I asked you to go to the dance with me. And you said you would think about it," Cruz said.

Tia said, "I did. I want to go to the

dance. But I want to go out of town more. Sorry, Cruz."

Cruz laughed.

Then he said, "Don't be sorry for me. It is your loss, not mine."

He could always get a date to the dance. He didn't have to go with Tia.

Tia said, "Maybe we could go out on a date sometime."

"Don't count on it," Cruz said. And he walked off.

How could Tia turn down a chance to date him?

But that was OK. He could always ask Ana. Or he could ask Paz.

Chapter 7

Cruz looked at Rey and Al. They looked back at him. He thought Rey was laughing. But he wasn't sure.

Was Rey laughing at him? Did Rey think he couldn't get a date?

Cruz could get a date. He knew that for sure.

Cruz looked for Ana. He told her he would call her and talk about the dance. So he would ask her now. He knew she would say yes.

He saw Ana. He walked over to her. But he didn't hurry.

Cruz said, "The spring dance is Friday night."

"I know," Ana said.

"Do you want to go with me?" Cruz asked.

"Yes, Cruz," Ana said.

Cruz knew Ana would say yes. Now he had a date. And Rey couldn't laugh at him.

Ana said, "But I can't go with you, Cruz. You are too late. I have a date with someone else."

Cruz couldn't believe it.

"Why did you make a date with someone else? I told you I would call you," Cruz said.

"Yes. You did say that. But I told you to call me that night. You said you would. But you didn't call me," Ana said.

Cruz said, "You knew I would ask you."

But that wasn't true.

Ana said, "No. I didn't know that, Cruz. So I didn't want to wait for you to ask me. You might not have asked me. And I didn't want to sit at home the night of the dance."

Cruz wished he hadn't waited so late to ask Ana. But he could always ask Paz.

He knew Paz wanted to go with him. And he told her he would call her about the dance.

Ana said, "I like to date you, Cruz. But next time ask me sooner, or don't ask me at all."

Cruz didn't want to make Ana mad. He might want to date her again.

So he said, "OK. I will ask you for a date sooner."

"Good," Ana said.

Then she went in the school.

Cruz looked at Rey and Al. They were still looking at him. And Rey was laughing.

Was Rey laughing at him?

Rey and Al walked over to Cruz.

Cruz knew why. They wanted to know who he was taking to the dance.

Cruz had to get a date for the dance, soon.

Chapter 8

Cruz looked for Paz. He saw her. She was with Bel. Bel was her best friend.

Bel's real name was Belinda. But her friends called her Bel.

Cruz didn't think Bel liked him. And he wished she were not with Paz. He didn't want to talk to Paz with Bel there. But he needed to talk to Paz now. So he went over to the two girls. And this time he did hurry.

Bel said, "I will go on to class, Paz. I will see you later."

"OK," Paz said.

Then Bel went in the school.

Cruz looked at Paz. He gave her a big smile.

Cruz said, "The spring dance is Friday night."

"I know," Paz said.

"Do you want to go to the dance with me?" Cruz asked.

He knew what Paz would say. She would say yes.

But that wasn't what Paz said.

"It's too late to ask me," Paz said.

"Why? Do you have a date?" Cruz asked.

"No," Paz said.

"So why is it too late to ask you? I told you I would call you," Cruz said.

"That was last week, Cruz. You didn't call me," Paz said.

"I am sorry I didn't call you last week, Paz. I was going to ask you to the dance then. But I didn't get a chance to call you," Cruz said.

That wasn't true. But Paz didn't know that.

"That is just it, Cruz. You said you would call me. But you didn't," Paz said.

"I could call you after school today. But I am asking you now. So how about it?" Cruz asked.

Paz didn't have a date. So he didn't think she would really turn him down.

"No," Paz said.

That surprised Cruz very much.

"Why? You don't have a date," Cruz said.

"You should have called me last week. You should have asked me then," Paz said.

"Forget about last week. That was then. This is now. And I am asking you to the dance now," Cruz said.

"And last week I would have said yes. But now I am saying no," Paz said.

Cruz wanted to walk off. He wanted to upset Paz. But he couldn't do that. He had to have a date to the dance.

There were other girls he would like to ask. But they might already have a date.

Cruz looked over at Rey and Al. They looked over at him. Rey was laughing. And Al had a big smile on his face.

Cruz had to have a date now. He knew Rey and Al would ask him who his date was. And he had to be able to tell them.

So he said, "Go to the dance with me, Paz. And I will ask you for a date sooner next time."

"No. And don't ask me for a date again," Paz said.

Cruz couldn't believe Paz said that. Just because he didn't call her last week.

"You don't mean that," he said.

He knew Paz liked him.

"Yes. I do," Paz said.

"But why?" Cruz asked.

"You say you will call. And then you don't call. I don't want a boyfriend who says he will call, then he doesn't call. I don't want a boyfriend who asks me very late. I want a boyfriend I can count on. And I can't count on you," Paz said.

Paz walked off. She went in the school.

Rey and Al hurried over to Cruz.

Rey said, "Who do you have a date with, Cruz? Is it Tia? Is it Ana? Is it Paz?"

"I will let you know later," Cruz said.

Rey looked at Al.

Rey said, "I told you all three girls said no. Cruz doesn't have a date to the dance."

"But I will have one soon," Cruz said.

But now Cruz wasn't sure he would have a date.

Rey laughed at Cruz.

Cruz had always thought it was OK to laugh at others. But now he didn't think that way.

He didn't like it when someone laughed at him. He didn't like it at all.

That wouldn't happen to him again. And he would make sure it didn't.

From now on he would ask girls sooner for a date. And he wouldn't tell a girl he would call her unless he meant to do it.

He would also work hard at baseball practice.

From now on, girls could count on him. His friends could count on him. And Coach Karr could count on him too.